EVERYONE LOVES
CUPCAKE

Kelly DiPucchio

pictures by
Eric Wight

FARRAR
STRAUS
GIROUX
NEW YORK

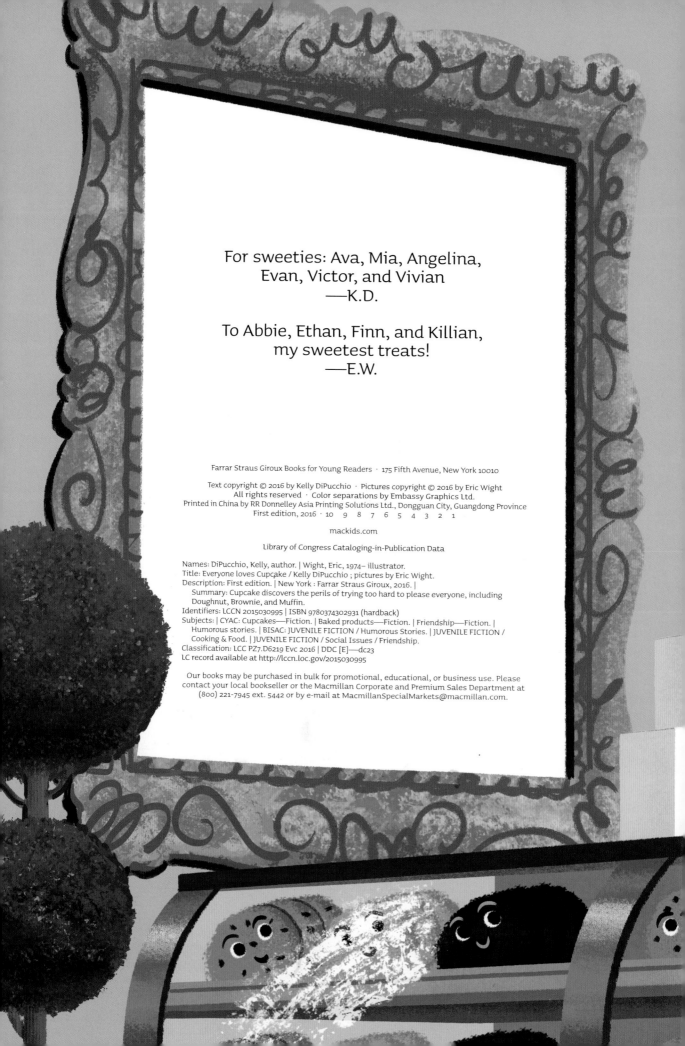

For sweeties: Ava, Mia, Angelina,
Evan, Victor, and Vivian
——K.D.

To Abbie, Ethan, Finn, and Killian,
my sweetest treats!
——E.W.

Farrar Straus Giroux Books for Young Readers · 175 Fifth Avenue, New York 10010

Text copyright © 2016 by Kelly DiPucchio · Pictures copyright © 2016 by Eric Wight
All rights reserved · Color separations by Embassy Graphics Ltd.
Printed in China by RR Donnelley Asia Printing Solutions Ltd., Dongguan City, Guangdong Province
First edition, 2016 · 10 9 8 7 6 5 4 3 2 1

mackids.com

Library of Congress Cataloging-in-Publication Data

Names: DiPucchio, Kelly, author. | Wight, Eric, 1974– illustrator.
Title: Everyone loves Cupcake / Kelly DiPucchio ; pictures by Eric Wight.
Description: First edition. | New York : Farrar Straus Giroux, 2016. |
     Summary: Cupcake discovers the perils of trying too hard to please everyone, including
     Doughnut, Brownie, and Muffin.
Identifiers: LCCN 2015030995 | ISBN 9780374302931 (hardback)
Subjects: | CYAC: Cupcakes—Fiction. | Baked products—Fiction. | Friendship—Fiction. |
     Humorous stories. | BISAC: JUVENILE FICTION / Humorous Stories. | JUVENILE FICTION /
     Cooking & Food. | JUVENILE FICTION / Social Issues / Friendship.
Classification: LCC PZ7.D6219 Evc 2016 | DDC [E]—dc23
LC record available at http://lccn.loc.gov/2015030995

Our books may be purchased in bulk for promotional, educational, or business use. Please
contact your local bookseller or the Macmillan Corporate and Premium Sales Department at
(800) 221-7945 ext. 5442 or by e-mail at MacmillanSpecialMarkets@macmillan.com.

Everyone loves Cupcake.

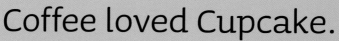
Coffee loved Cupcake.

Brownie loved Cupcake.

Angel Food Cake loved Cupcake, too, but she didn't count because Angel Food Cake loved **everyone**.

Cupcake worked hard at getting her friends to like her.

Everywhere she went, Cupcake
tried her best to impress.

Her smile was brilliant.

Her wave was impeccable.

She even wore a tiara.

Everyone loves a tiara.

Cupcake worried a lot about what everyone thought, so she worked **extra** hard at being **extra** perfect.

She fussed.

She fixed.

She fussed
and fixed
some more.

And she **never** stopped talking about how perfect things were.

After I rescued these sweet little guys from a burning oven, I alphabetized the spice rack!

Cinnamon Bun rolled his eyes.
Turnover walked away.
And Muffin blew his top.

Even worse, they pretended she wasn't there.

Cupcake sniffed. She was
feeling crummy and all alone.

Finally, Cookie offered her some advice.

Cupcake smiled.

Cookie blushed. Everyone
loves a smart cookie.

She paused, took a deep breath,
and then blurted out . . .

Everyone gasped!

The room went quiet.

And then everyone cheered! Cupcake's friends took turns sharing their true feelings.

Indeed, nobody is perfect.
Not even Angel Food Cake.

Yep, everyone loves Cupcake.